IN THE
Tummy of a Whale

LaPapaLePere Publishing

First paperback edition published April 2020 by LaPapaLePere Publishing

ISBN 978-1-8380232-0-1 (paperback)
ISBN 978-1-8380232-1-8 (eBook)

Published by LaPapaLePere Publishing
www.lapapalepere.co.uk

IN THE
Tummy of a Whale

WRITTEN BY ANTHONY COLLINS
ILLUSTRATED BY REBECCA COLLINS

Jacob Smee set off to sea
in a boat he had made out of twigs from a tree.
With waters calm and sun ablaze
he checked his notes for a relevant phrase.

"Ship ahoy!" the young lad hailed.

"Shiver me timbers!" he'd got this nailed.

Under the stars with the moon his light
Jacob read until midnight;
then fell into the deepest sleep
where adventures take place, with secrets to keep.

T'was then that the wind blew up from the north
and Jacob's story took a different course.
The little boat climbed and fell in the waves,
a sea full of holes and watery graves.

The rain fell so hard it woke up our captain.
Oh, how he wished he was more tightly strapped in.

On the surface came fins,
and the sharks arrived.
Poor Jacob was certain he wouldn't survive.
"I smell your fear," the first shark said.
"You should've stayed
tucked up warm in your bed."

The second shark laughed, then suddenly froze
as Jacob punched him hard, on the nose.

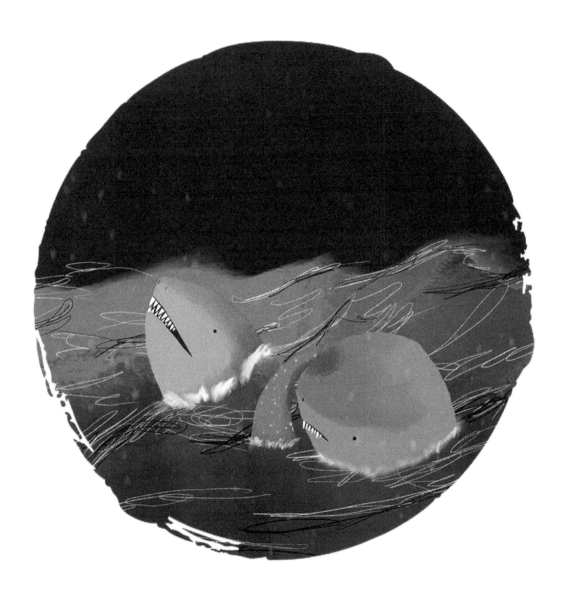

"You don't scare me," our hero announced.
But right at that moment the little boat bounced.
The largest of waves had crashed on the deck,
Jacob was in it right up to his neck.

The poor boy paddled as fast as he could,
but when it comes to swimming sharks are quite good.
"And so this is it," poor Jacob cried,
"not a bad way for a captain to die."

The last thing he saw were the teeth of the shark.
He squeezed his eyes shut and it all went dark.
No sound, no light, and no awful pain,
perhaps these two sharks are playing a game?
Then came a voice much warmer and kind,
"Sharks taste like apples and cold bacon rind."

Jacob slowly opened his eyes,
and prayed that he'd see the star-filled sky.
But instead all around was a blanket of dark.
Was Jacob now trapped in the gut of a shark?
Although it was smelly and terribly gloomy
this shark's innards were surprisingly roomy.
Stretching his arms, no side could he touch.
This made no sense, it's all double-dutch.

"Are you warm enough?" the voice came again,
"if there's plankton around, I'll try and abstain.
For if I were to swallow more than I oughta,
you might end up shivering back in the water."

Jacob decided he had to be brave
and discover who owns this gigantic cave.
"Excuse me, kind sir," he nervously inquired,
"am I still alive, or have I expired?"

A huge hearty laugh filled the space like a cloak.
Jacob assumed it was some kind of joke.
"I'll tell you in song which will make a nice change."
The voice cleared his throat and then a tune came.

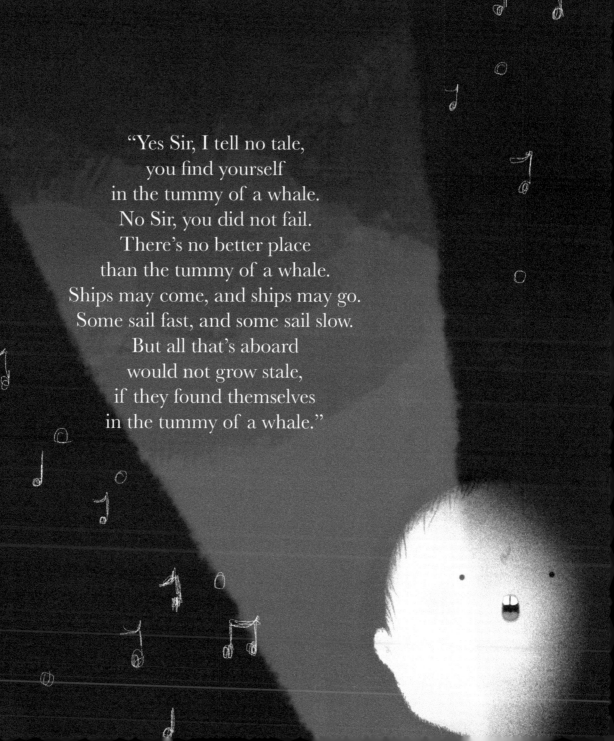

"Yes Sir, I tell no tale,
you find yourself
in the tummy of a whale.
No Sir, you did not fail.
There's no better place
than the tummy of a whale.
Ships may come, and ships may go.
Some sail fast, and some sail slow.
But all that's aboard
would not grow stale,
if they found themselves
in the tummy of a whale."

After careful thought, Jacob had a suggestion
and posed his host a difficult question.
"Would there be any chance of getting some light,
something quite gentle, nothing too bright?
Then I can verify your little story
and possibly check your guts inventory."

All at once right after that wish,
the tummy was filled with luminous fish.

"Is that better now?"
the whale inquired.
Jacob stood speechless,
utterly inspired.
Before him, a trove
like a treasure filled chest.
All things that the whale
just couldn't digest.

"This is amazing," Jacob finally said.
"How did you swallow a king sized bed?"
Feeling quite tired the boy gave it a try
and soon shut his eyes and whispered, "Goodnight."

As morning arrived breakfast was dished.
"I hope you like fish, cos that's all that there is."
Jacob tucked into a plate of cod lips,
"I don't suppose you've got sauce and some chips?"

The whale thought he may once
have swallowed a fridge,
from that time he got lost
at the Golden Gate Bridge.

Jacob spied it next to a full suit of armour,
in front of a bike and stuffed Turkish llama.

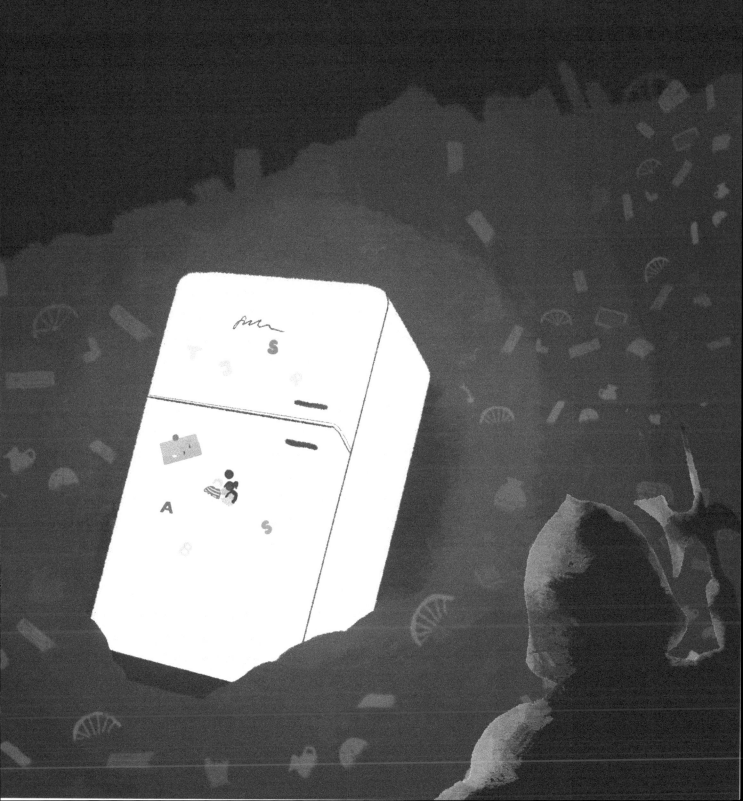

He opened the fridge and gave the happiest cry,
"Two pickled eggs and the freshest pork pie!"

With breakfast now done,
Jacob wanted to follow
the trail of things that the whale
had once swallowed.

He called them all out
to the whale just in case
he'd forgotten the things
still stuck down in this place.

After the fridge, the bike, and the bed,
the armour was pointing at an old wooden shed.
The door was wide open, revealing inside
an old vintage mower and a toddlers slide.

Further along, was a chest of drawers
with handles made from animals claws.
Buckets, cans, and oily drums,
barrels of whiskies, brandies, and rums.

The whale requested that, although he was young,
would Jacob pour some brandy onto his tongue?
"Of course!" said the boy and duly obliged.
The whale gave a swallow and a satisfied sigh.

Beyond some gems, a mirror, and clocks,
a shiny silver jewellery box.
It gleamed so brightly and called aloud
for Jacob to look, if he were allowed?

"Ah yes," said the whale, "I remember this well,
I rescued it when the Titanic fell.
Perhaps when you open and look inside
it will help mend your heart and be your guide."

With a turn of the key and a lift of the lid
Jacob found the treasure that the jewellery box hid.

A photograph of a mother and child,
the boy fast asleep while the mother smiled.

"Now you know where to go, at any cost.
Jacob my friend you're no longer lost.

The things you've seen here reflect my days,
I've collected my memories in so many ways."

And all of a sudden the whale's jaw opened wide,
the blue of the ocean appeared outside.
At Jacob's side, an old bath sat.
"Climb in," said the whale,
"you'll be fine in that."

The rushing waves grabbed the makeshift craft,
and the whale let out a hearty laugh.

"Now go and collect
some things of your own
and don't share them unless
you're afraid and alone.
It's obvious, the key
to remembering well
is to **keep on collecting
and don't ever dwell.**"

Jacob and the bath were spat out to sea.
The whale disappeared without being seen.

The wind carried the boy to the shore by his home,
where his mother was waiting, tired and alone.

That night as he sat and looked out to the ocean,
Jacob imagined that beautiful potion

had gifted him a life-long tale
once told to him in the tummy of a whale.

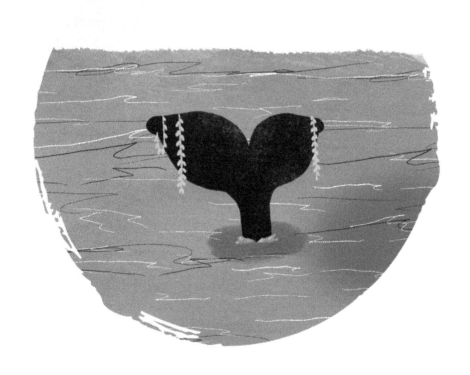

Lightning Source UK Ltd.
Milton Keynes UK
UKHW051213300420
362563UK00005B/46